Cinderella's Fairy Merry Christmas

By Andrea Posner-Sanchez
Illustrated by Elisa Marrucchi

Random House 🏠 New York

Copyright © 2009 Disney Enterprises, Inc. All rights reserved. Published in the United States by Random House Children's Books, a division of Random House, Inc., 1745 Broadway, New York, NY 10019, and in Canada by Random House of Canada Limited, Toronto, in conjunction with Disney Enterprises, Inc. Random House and the colophon are registered trademarks of Random House, Inc.
Library of Congress Control Number: 2009920759
ISBN: 978-0-7364-2622-0
www.randomhouse.com/kids
Printed in the United States of America
10 9
First Edition

"Look! It's snowing!" Cinderella announced to Gus and Jaq. Christmas was just a day away, and the princess was very excited about her first holiday with the Prince. "It's going to be just as I've always dreamed!"

Cinderella looked all around the castle's grand living room. "I can put a wreath on the door, some stockings on the mantel, a tree by the window—"

"Tree too big for me, Gus-Gus, and Cinderelly to carry," interrupted little Jaq.

"You're right," Cinderella agreed. "We'll have to get some help."

Just then, a burst of sparkling fairy dust swirled around the room. "Did somebody call for help?" It was Cinderella's fairy godmother! "*Bibbidi-bobbidi-boo* doesn't just work on gowns and pumpkins, you know. I can make any occasion extra special," she told the princess.

The princess was thrilled to see her old friend. After a warm hug, the Fairy Godmother asked, "So what's this I hear about a tree?"

Cinderella explained that she wanted a nice little Christmas tree set up in front of the window.

"Leave everything to me, dearie," the Fairy Godmother said as she raised her wand.

Cinderella and the mice headed for the stairs. "We'll be back soon with the ornaments."

"I know the Prince will just love our handmade ornaments," Cinderella told her mouse friends.

Together they created decorations with odds and ends the mice had found around the castle. They cut snowflakes out of white paper. They used strings of beads for garland. And they glued ribbons to pinecones.

Gus and Jaq held up a big star made from shiny paper. "Don't forget this, Cinderelly!"

"You can both help me put the star at the very top," Cinderella told them. "Let's see if the tree is ready."

Cinderella and the mice went back downstairs. They couldn't believe what they saw!

"Ta-dah!" announced the Fairy Godmother.

The biggest, tallest tree imaginable was standing in the living room. It was covered from top to bottom in gold and diamond ornaments.

"Oh, my," Cinderella whispered. "It's . . . it's lovely, but . . ."

"Is the size wrong?" asked the Fairy Godmother. "I can make it bigger."

"No, no, no. That's not it," answered Cinderella quickly. "I was actually picturing something smaller. And simpler."

"Like the ornaments Cinderelly made," added Jaq.

The Fairy Godmother knew just what to do. With a wave of her wand, the huge tree disappeared and a smaller one took its place.

"It's perfect," Cinderella told her, clapping her hands with delight. "Let's hang the ornaments and place the star on top."

"Now we can work on the gifts for the Prince," Cinderella suggested The Fairy Godmother said some magic spells. *Poof!* A diamond-covered saddle and a golden pair of riding boots appeared.

"They're very shiny and beautiful," Cinderella commented, "but the most special gifts are ones that come from the heart."

"The Prince likes cookies," said Jaq.

"Me too!" added Gus.

The princess thought that was a great idea. Everyone went to the royal kitchen to bake cookies for the Prince.

"Ta-dah!" announced the Fairy Godmother as she held up an enormous cookie.

"I'm worried that might give the Prince a tummyache," Cinderella said sweetly. "Perhaps these are more his size." She handed the Fairy Godmother one of the cookies she and the mice had baked.

"Mmm! I didn't know nonmagical cookies could taste so good!" the Fairy Godmother exclaimed.

Later, when Cinderella went off to make another present for the Prince, the Fairy Godmother decided to decorate the rest of the castle. Luckily, Gus and Jaq were there to keep an eye on things.

After a long, busy day, everyone slept well that night. They all had sweet Christmas dreams.

On Christmas morning, the Prince and princess rushed downstairs
to find Jaq and Gus singing carols.

The living room was decorated just as Cinderella had planned.
"Everything looks beautiful," the Prince told her.

The Prince picked up a present from under the tree and handed it to the princess. "I made this myself," he told her. "I hope you like it."

Cinderella passed a box tied with ribbon to the Prince. "And I made this just for you."

They opened their gifts at the same time. The Prince received a portrait of his horse. Cinderella got a painting of her darling mouse friends.

"I love it!" they said together.

Christmas in the castle was even better than Cinderella had imagined. And the most wonderful part of all was that she was able to spend the day with the people—and mice—she loved most.